R0085249068

08/2017

D0810596

DISCARD

Nikki & Deja

by Karen English

Illustrated by Laura Freeman

Houghton Mifflin Harcourt
Boston ✳ New York

To all the Nikkis and Dejas who've passed through my classroom
— K.E.
To Jimmy
— L.F.

The text of this book is set in 14-point Warnock Pro Caption.
The illustrations are executed digitally.

The Library of Congress has cataloged the hardcover edition as follows:
English, Karen.
Niki and Deja / by Karen English; illustrated by Laura Freeman.
p. cm.
Summary: When an arrogant new girl comes to school,
third-graders and best friends Nikki and Deja decide to form a club that
would exclude her but find the results not what they expected.
[1. Best friends – Fiction. 2. Friendship – Fiction. 3. Schools – Fiction. 4. Clubs – Fiction.]
1. Freeman, Laura, ill. II. Title. PZ7.E7232Ni 2007
[Fic] – dc22 2006030974

ISBN: 978-0-618-75238-6 hardcover
ISBN: 978-0-547-13362-1 paperback

Manufactured in U.S.A.
EBM 10 9 8 7 6 5
4500632821

– Contents –

What Did You Do to My Hair?

Nikki and Deja are best friends. They live next door to each other. On Saturday they sit on Deja's couch watching cartoons. Soon Nikki grows tired of *The Mouse Queen* and says, "Let's walk to the store."

"I can't," Deja says. "My hair's not combed." She plucks at Bear's fur. Bear is her favorite stuffed animal. Deja's hair sticks out all over, just like Bear's fur. "And Auntie Dee can't comb it 'cause she's working in the garden right now."

Just then, the garage door to the kitchen slams and Auntie Dee passes through the room carrying a tray of seedlings to the backyard. "You're not spending the whole morning in front of that TV," she announces.

After she leaves, Deja says, "See? She's too busy to comb my hair right now."

"Let me comb it," Nikki says.

"You don't know how."

"Yes, I do. I know how to comb hair now."

Deja looks at Nikki as if she doesn't believe her.

"I comb my little cousin's hair all the time," Nikki says.

Deja gets off the couch and runs to the bathroom. Soon she comes back with her comb and brush and ten ball barrettes. She sets them on the coffee table. "I want the pink ones in the front, the blue in the middle, and the purple on the bottom," she says, scooting down onto the floor.

Nikki picks up the comb and tries to pull it through Deja's hair.

"Ow!" Deja cries.

"I'll use the brush first," Nikki says quickly.

"Everybody knows you're *supposed* to use the brush first, Nikki."

Nikki looks at the barrettes and realizes she hasn't learned how to make them work yet. She brushes until she thinks she can pull the comb through, but it gets stuck again. She gives it a tug.

"Ow!" Deja cries. "That hurts!"

Nikki puts the comb down. She won't comb anymore. She'll just brush. Then she remembers that she hasn't learned how to braid. So she decides to put bunches of hair in the barrettes. But she doesn't really know how to do that, either.

Deja reaches up and touches her head.

"This doesn't feel right!" She jumps up and runs to the bathroom to check it in the mirror. Then she comes running back.

"Look what you did to my hair!"

"I like it . . . ," Nikki says weakly.

"It doesn't look like it's supposed to!"

"Yes, it does."

"It doesn't."

Deja flops down on the couch. She slips her thumb into her mouth and turns back to *The Mouse Queen,* her favorite cartoon. Deja won't let anyone except Nikki see her sucking her thumb. She knows Nikki won't laugh. Nikki slides over next to Deja on the couch. There isn't anything about Deja that Nikki would laugh at, and there isn't anything about Nikki that Deja would laugh at.

After a while, Deja takes her thumb out of her mouth and says, "I'm tired of cartoons. Let's go outside. I don't need my hair combed for that."

New Neighbors

They settle on Nikki's front porch to watch the happenings on their street. Bear sits on the steps between them. Watching their neighbors on Fulton Street is one of their favorite things to do on Saturday mornings. Mr. Robinson, next door, putters in his yard. Bobby, across the street, washes his car. Vianda, next door to Bobby, practices drill steps with her high school friends. Nikki and Deja even like to watch the mailman make his way up and down their block.

"I bet we could do that," Deja says, pointing to Vianda. "It's kind of like cheerleading— without the jumping up and down. It looks easy."

Nikki watches for a while. It doesn't look easy to her.

Nikki's mother opens the screen door and sticks her head out. "Nikki, you need to come in and clean your room."

"Can I stay out for fifteen more minutes?"

"Fifteen minutes," she says. "No longer."

Nikki watches Deja as she tries to imitate Vianda and her friends. She does a little shuffle and slide. Then she looks at Nikki, seemingly very proud of herself.

But Nikki isn't paying attention anymore. A big green moving van is rumbling down Fulton Street. It pulls up to the empty house three doors down with a loud screech. Deja watches, too. "New neighbors," they say at the same time and slap palms.

The van's back doors swing open, a ramp clangs to the curb, and one of the moving men rolls down a big blue bureau. Nikki and Deja watch as chairs and tables and sofas and boxes and . . . a dollhouse! . . . are carried into the house.

"Kids," they say together and slap palms again.

Nikki reaches for the special pouch she

wears around her neck. She takes out the pad and pencil she keeps inside it and starts to write down what she sees.

Deja glances over at her. Nikki likes making lists.

They watch the movers unload more boxes and a smart pink bedroom set with a canopy bed. Then the movers unload a trampoline!

Nikki and Deja stare. They look at each other, speechless. No one they know has a trampoline.

"How do you spell trampoline?" Nikki asks, tapping her notepad with her pencil.

"*You're* the spelling bee champ," Deja says.

At that point, a big black car pulls up behind the moving van. A man, a lady, and a little girl who looks the same age as Nikki and Deja climb out. Nikki and Deja stare hard at the girl, willing her to look their way. She doesn't. She just fiddles with the tip of her very long braid and stops to peer down into one of the boxes.

"Her hair is long," Deja says.

Nikki leans her head back to make her own two braids look longer. "Deja, whose hair is longer? Mine or hers?"

Deja doesn't even have to look at Nikki. "Her hair is way longer."

Just then, the new girl straightens and glances over at them. Ever so slightly, she rolls her eyes and walks into the house. The door closes behind her.

"Did you see that?" Deja says. "She rolled her eyes at us!"

"Yeah!" Nikki says. She can't *believe* that new girl rolled her eyes at them.

"Who cares about her old ugly canopy bed?"

Nikki wasn't thinking about the bed. But now that Deja brings it up, she realizes she did want to see it close up. "Yeah," she says weakly.

"Let's have a club and make sure that girl is not in it," Deja says. "Let's make her sorry she rolled her eyes at us!"

Ms. Shelby Shops at Big Barn

Nikki's dad pulls into a parking space in front of the supermarket. He always takes Nikki food shopping on Sunday afternoons so Nikki's mom can have some time to herself.

Now he turns around and gives Nikki and Deja, in the back seat, one of his no-nonsense looks. "Listen, when we get into Big Barn, I don't want to hear any begging. Are we clear on that?" They nod. But Nikki knows she can always beg for a few extra goodies.

"Stay close," he says as they enter the store. He always says that, but Nikki also knows he'll let her go to the magazine rack, as long as Deja's with her. She and Deja love to look at the decorator magazines and plan their future houses. Deja is going to be a decorator when she grows up, and Nikki's going to be a newspaper reporter.

"Can we go to the magazine rack for just a little while?"

Nikki's dad squints, thinking. He always does that before giving permission.

"Ten minutes," he says, then walks off frowning at the long list Nikki's mom has given him. Nikki and Deja about-face, mouths pressed in secret smiles, and head straight for the magazines.

"You see, Nikki, when I grow up and have lots and lots of money, my bedroom is going to have a lavender color scheme," Deja says. Nikki thinks about this—about Deja having lots of money.

Just then, someone at the end of the cereal aisle catches Nikki's eye: *It's Ms. Shelby, their teacher . . . pushing a shopping cart in Big Barn!*

"Ms. Shelby!" she whispers excitedly.

"What?" Deja says, looking up from her magazine.

Nikki points. "There's Ms. Shelby!"

At the end of the aisle, they see their teacher

peering down at a piece of paper in her hand.

"She shops at Big Barn!" Deja says in a near whisper. "Wonder what she's buying?"

Automatically, Nikki pulls out her notebook and turns to a fresh page. Ms. Shelby leaves her cart and turns the corner to go down the Mexican/Asian food aisle.

"Quick, let's see what she's got in her cart," Deja says.

"She'll see us," Nikki says.

"Then we'll just say, 'Hi, Ms. Shelby. How ya doin'?'"

"You know you're not going to say that, Deja."

"Come on . . ." Deja is already leading the way.

Ms. Shelby's shopping cart is pushed aside to make room for the carts of other shoppers. They gaze down into it, Nikki with her pencil poised.

"Ten low-fat yogurts," Nikki says.

"She must be on a diet," Deja says.

"No, my mom buys low-fat, and she's not on a diet."

"Whole-wheat bread," Deja says.

"Coffee beans."

They scoot back to the far end of the aisle, out of sight. When Ms. Shelby returns to her cart, they follow her at a safe distance. For ten minutes they watch Ms. Shelby place items in her cart, slowly and thoughtfully. Nikki records everything, not caring about the spelling. She plans to fix that later. When it's time to go and find her daddy, she's recorded fifteen items, including herb-scented shampoo, hand lotion, toothpaste, and a new toothbrush.

"I never thought of Ms. Shelby brushing her teeth," Deja says.

Later, Nikki and Deja sit on Deja's porch and look at each item on the list. They are amazed over and over that their teacher eats diet TV dinners and washes her hair with herb-scented shampoo.

4

Stupid Antonia

On Monday morning before journal writing, right while Ms. Shelby (who probably brushed her teeth that morning with her new toothbrush) is busy with attendance, Mr. Brown, the principal, walks in. Their new neighbor is right behind him. She stands by the door and looks over the class with what Nikki decides is clearly a sneer.

"Room Ten, today you're getting a new student." Mr. Brown smiles. "This is Antonia."

Antonia doesn't smile.

The class stares. Antonia is carrying a see-through backpack and a red plaid lunch bag. "Hi, Antonia," everyone finally says together.

"Hi," she says, very, very quietly.

"You may find a seat, Antonia," Ms. Shelby says. Mr. Brown leaves, and Antonia chooses the empty seat next to Deja, even though there is a perfectly good seat next to Ralph. Carefully, she unpacks her backpack. Ms. Shelby hasn't assigned her a cubby yet. She takes out a pink plastic pencil case and opens it. Nikki sees sharpened pencils and a new pink eraser and a small stapler and a ruler. Then Antonia turns her pencil box toward Deja so that she can see inside. Deja looks surprised, as if she doesn't know what to think.

"She thinks she's so cute," Nikki hears Ayanna whisper nearby.

Ms. Shelby steps away from the board, revealing that morning's journal topic: *My Favorite Day of the Week.* "Here, Antonia," she says, handing her a brand-new cream-colored notebook. "This is what you'll use for your journal."

All heads bend toward their blank pages. Some of the children begin writing right away. A few take time to stare into space. Others hope to avoid beginning their work by finding something else to do. Nikki dives right in. She notices Antonia does, too. When Nikki looks up, she sees Deja drawing rainbows in her journal. Nikki knows drawing helps Deja think. Even though Ms. Shelby (who eats low-fat yogurt!) might look over her shoulder on her slow circuit around the class and announce, "*Someone* isn't following directions."

When the recess bell rings, Ms. Shelby says, "Pass your journals up and then show me you're ready to go outside."

Antonia turns in her journal, then folds her hands and looks straight ahead. Some kids in the class seem not to have heard Ms. Shelby. There are one or two talkers who are spoiling it for their entire rows, including Nikki's.

"Row Three—you look like you're ready. Please line up. In fact, you may go out now." Ms. Shelby makes a show of looking at the other rows. Ms. Shelby never has to yell. She just waits.

Deja is in Row Three. So is Antonia. She takes a red-and-blue-striped jump rope out of her see-through backpack. It has musical handles that jingle like bells. Deja and Antonia go outside with their row. Nikki watches the door close behind them, then sits up extra straight. Finally, her row is called.

Once outside, she stops in her tracks. Deja is jumping rope with Antonia!

"Nikki, come jump with us," Deja cries.

As soon as Nikki reaches them, Antonia shoves the ends of the rope into Nikki and Deja's hands. "I go first," she says.

Nikki and Deja turn while Antonia jumps and jumps and jumps. Nikki's arm grows tired, and so does Deja's. Finally, Antonia must grow tired, too, because she jumps on the rope.

"You're out," Deja cries. "I'm in!"

"No, I'm not." Antonia looks at Nikki. "You pulled the rope."

"I did not!"

"You did, too. I get to jump again."

Nikki and Deja turn the rope again. And turn, and turn, and turn until Antonia jumps on it again. "Out," Deja says.

"I am not. You can't turn right." She stops to catch her breath. "I go again."

"I'm not turning anymore."

"Then you can't play with my jump rope."

"So?" Deja says, frowning.

Antonia yanks the tinkly handle away from Deja.

Deja looks down at her empty hand.

Antonia yanks the other handle away from Nikki.

Nikki shrugs. She feels good shrugging. "I don't even want to play with your stupid rope." She looks at Deja to see if Deja feels the same way.

"Me, neither," Deja says. "I don't want to jump with your dumb rope." She slips her hand in Nikki's. "Come on, Nikki. Let's go play four square before the bell rings."

"Fine, then," Antonia calls after them. "I was going to let you come over after school and jump on my trampoline! But now I've changed my mind!"

Nikki feels Deja hesitate just a little bit. She tugs on Deja's arm.

"Who cares?" Deja yells back, without turning around. "I don't even want to jump on your stupid trampoline!"

Nikki is filled with satisfaction. She knows Deja would love to jump on that trampoline. But Deja is back to being Nikki's one and only best friend and no one else's.

"Nikki," Deja says, "we need to start our club."

"What kind of club?"

"I don't know yet," Deja says. "But we need a club, and we need to keep stupid Antonia out of it."

That sounds like a good idea to Nikki. Thinking about their future club, they walk around the schoolyard, arm in arm, until the freeze bell rings. Then all the kids on the playground stop in place while the ball monitors walk around collecting balls and ropes and Hula-Hoops. Soon the second bell rings, and everyone makes a mad dash for their lines.

Nikki and Deja look around to see if Mrs. Miller's and Mr. Beaumont's third-grade classes are completely and quietly in their lines. Mr. Brown has promised a pizza party for the class from each grade level that's first to get in line completely and quietly the most times in one month. Mr. Beaumont's class is winning so far, with ten days to go. But today they see that Robert Foster from Mrs. Miller's class is still at the water fountain, and Anna Martinez from Mr. Beaumont's class is just coming out of the bathroom.

Mr. Brown, from his place in front of the line-up area, looks over at Ms. Shelby and gives

her the thumbs-up. The kids from Room Ten smile, but they know not to whoop and holler with glee. They know to remain quiet and orderly all the way to the classroom.

5

Deja's Idea

"A drill club," Deja says the next day. "A drill club for those who can really drill." They are playing jacks on Deja's front porch. Auntie Dee is preparing dinner, and through the open window they can hear her singing along with the radio. Deja's Auntie Dee has a really good voice.

"Sixies," Deja says. She bounces the ball and swoops up six jacks at a time, over and over, until she's scooped up every last one on the floor. "Sevensies."

Nikki watches, secretly hoping Deja will mess up. Deja is good at jacks. She's better than Nikki. No such luck. She whizzes through sevensies, too.

"Eightsies," Deja says. "Everyone *thinks* they can drill."

"Maybe because it's like dancing, but everyone does the same thing in a line together," Nikki offers.

A loud car motor revs up across the street. They look over at Bobby backing out of his driveway in his shiny black car. Bobby loves that car, Nikki thinks.

"That car would look better if it was lavender," Deja says.

Nikki has never seen a lavender car. She doesn't think there are any, but she doesn't tell Deja this.

Deja gets back to the subject. "The problem is, drilling *is* a lot like dancing, Nikki. You have to have rhythm. And not everyone has rhythm."

Nikki wonders if she has rhythm. She wonders if she has as much rhythm as Deja.

"We'll each pick two girls. You pick two, and I pick two." Deja swoops up eight jacks, but one falls out of her hand at the last second. Nikki tries not to smile.

"My turn," Nikki says.

Deja smiles as if she doesn't care, because

Nikki's only on twosies. Nikki doesn't like it when Deja gets that smug look on her face. It's the same look she gets when Ms. Shelby has to step into the hall for a minute to speak with another teacher and lets Deja write down the names of the talkers. Or when it's her turn to be line leader.

Nikki throws the jacks down. She frowns. She's thrown them so that each jack is far from the other jacks. She bounces the ball and tries to scoop up just two jacks and then catch the ball before it bounces more than once. Her hand isn't quick enough.

"My turn," Deja says. She shakes the jacks in her hand and says, "I'm thinking of asking Keisha and ChiChi. They can dance really good." She throws out the jacks. She has to do eightsies all over again, since she messed up before. She bounces the ball, and scoops up eight jacks easily. "Who are you picking, Nikki?"

Nikki doesn't know yet. She plans to make a list as soon as she gets home, then study her list before she decides. "Maybe Rosario for one. . . . I'm not sure who else. I have to think about it." She wonders what Deja means by "dance really good."

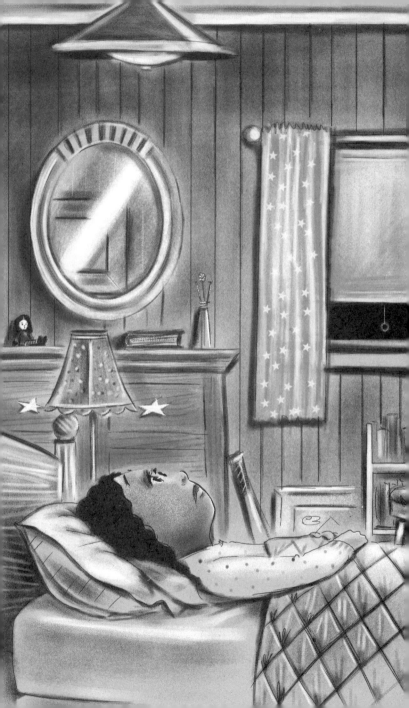

* * *

That night when Nikki goes to bed, she thinks about the drill club while staring up at the ceiling. Maybe she can practice and get "good" before the tryouts Deja is organizing. For some reason, she doesn't think so. Perhaps because of what she's always suspected about herself: *She has no rhythm.*

Invitations

Deja skips down her front steps the next morning and joins Nikki on the walk in front of her house. Deja has a big grin on her face. She has it all planned, she tells Nikki.

She digs in her book bag. "Look." Deja holds up four hearts cut out of red construction paper. She's very proud of her creations. "Invitations to our tryouts." Deja hands Nikki two. "Two for you, and two for me. And none for *Antonia*."

At that moment, Antonia comes out of her house and skips down her front steps to the car waiting in the driveway.

They look at Antonia sitting in the back seat as her father pulls out onto Fulton Street. She ignores them.

"She is *soooo* stuck up," Deja says. Then she puts her finger in her open mouth and makes a gagging sound.

Nikki follows suit. They laugh and laugh. Finally, Nikki looks down at the two lopsided hearts covered in clumps of glitter. Too much glue, she thinks.

You have been chosen to try
out for our Drill Team club.
Tryouts are at recess in
back of the handball court.
If you're late, you don't get in.

"You got the best ones. I kind of messed up on mine," Deja says. "I misspelled 'recess' and had to cross out the extra *c*. I couldn't erase because I used black marker." She looks down at her own hearts.

Nikki bets Deja wishes she hadn't used marker. Nikki looks at Deja's invitations. How many times has she told Deja it's better to write in pencil first and *then* go over it in marker? Marker can't be erased.

"Deja, why do we have to have tryouts at recess? Everybody's going to be looking."

"So?"

"They might laugh."

"Nobody's going to laugh. They're going to want to get in our club." Deja grabs Nikki by the hand to hurry her along. Deja must be anxious to get to school and start spreading the news about the tryouts, Nikki thinks. Before they look both ways to cross the street, they watch Vianda let out her cat, Bianca. Bianca trots across the street as if she knows where she's going and she's in a hurry to get there.

During morning journal writing, Deja waits until Ms. Shelby turns her back to the class to post that week's spelling words. Then Deja passes an invitation to Keisha, who sits right behind her. ChiChi, on the other side of the room, is busy staring at the topic for morning journal: *My Best Friend.* Deja can't get her attention. She folds the invitation into an airplane and sails it to ChiChi. It lands under her desk. ChiChi looks down at it, then reaches to pick it up. After she studies the globs of glitter on the front, she turns it over. Finally, she looks at Deja and smiles. Deja smiles back.

Nikki looks around the room. She takes out

her notebook and looks at her list. When she looks up, she spies Antonia sneaking sunflower seeds out of a package in her desk. Antonia slips one into her mouth and then carefully extracts the chewed-up shell. Then, she places the shell in the tray inside her desk meant to hold pencils.

Nikki wonders if she should raise her hand and tell Ms. Shelby. No. People might think she's a tattletale. She watches for a while, then returns to her list.

There are ten names. Of all the girls on the list, Nikki likes Rosario and Melinda best. She gets up to exchange her pencil for a sharpened one in the pencil can, even though hers is still sharp. On her way to the front of the room, she passes one invitation to Melinda, who sits in the front of her row, and then gives one to Rosario, who sits near the teacher's desk. When she sits back down, she looks first at Melinda, who's busy running her fingers over the glitter. Then she looks at Rosario, who's reading the other side of the heart. Ms. Shelby turns around and looks straight at Nikki. Nikki quickly gets back to her journal.

On the other side of the room, Nikki sees

Deja dive into her topic. Nikki begins to write as well:

My Best Friend is a girl named Deja. She lives next door to me which is good because I can go over to her house and she can come over to my house very easy. She doesn't have any brothers or sisters and I don't either so we are like sisters. She has her Auntie Dee and she's like Deja's mother because she's lived with her Auntie Dee since she was a baby. My mother and father are her pretend uncle and auntie. Deja's favorite color is lavender and mine is blue. I'm good at math and making lists and writing about the people who live on our block. Deja is good at decorating.

The End

P.S. Deja says lavender reminds her of spring time and warm weather.

7

Tryouts

When it's time for recess and everyone goes outside, Deja and Nikki head to the handball court, with the girls who are going to try out trailing behind them.

Deja has them all line up—even Nikki. She studies them and squints her eyes. Then she moves them around into a new arrangement. "Hmm," she says. Next, she puts on her serious face. "Okay. If you want to be in our Drill Team Club—"

"Who else is in it?" Rosario wants to know.

"Me and Nikki," Deja says.

"That's all?" Melinda asks. She sounds as if she expected more people. Even ChiChi, who never says very much, has a disappointed look on her face.

"Well," Deja says, "if we're good, everyone's going to want to be in our club."

Rosario frowns. She chews at a fingernail. Keisha starts gazing across the yard toward the tetherball game she's missing. She's very good at tetherball.

"Okay, everyone. Pay attention. I'm going to show you this routine I saw these high school girls doing. One of them lives across the street. And me and Nikki, we see them all the time practicing. Huh, Nikki?"

Nikki, who has been staring off at some girls jumping rope, nods.

"Then," Deja continues, "after you watch me, I'm going to see who can do it by themselves."

"And what if we can't?" Rosario says. She seems bored.

Deja looks at Rosario as if she thinks Rosario is a troublemaker. "Well, I think you can. Come on. Watch me."

Everyone watches while Deja, who's always been a good dancer, begins some fast shuffles, stomps, twists, and arm waving.

Too complicated, Nikki thinks. *Nobody's going to be able to do that*. She can't remember how many stomps, when to shuffle, or which way she should twist. Impossible.

But when Deja starts again, everyone follows along. When she finishes, everyone lines up beside her and does what Deja does again. The more they follow along, the more fun they seem to be having. Except Nikki. She has a hard time keeping up. She can't remember what to do or think as fast as the other girls. They go right, she goes left. They turn, and she's still looking around to see what everyone is doing. Then she tries to catch up. When they stop to take a breath, Deja is looking at her and frowning.

"Okay," Deja says. "Now I want everyone to do the drill on their own while I watch."

"No," says Nikki.

"You have to, Nikki. You have to show me you can do it on your own."

"I don't feel like it," Nikki says.

"What's wrong with you? Why are you acting like this?"

"Acting like what?" Nikki knows what Deja means, but she has no answer that she wants to admit to.

"Why don't you want to?"

The freeze bell cuts Deja off. Mr. Brown strolls up to the front of the line-up area of the playground with a clipboard and searching eyes. Finally, the second bell rings, and most of the kids walk to their places to wait for their teachers to pick them up. Once in line, Deja and Nikki check Mrs. Miller's class and Mr. Beaumont's class. Unfortunately, everyone seems to be where they're supposed to be. Room Ten is still in second place, behind Mr. Beaumont's class.

"Nikki," Deja begins slowly as they walk home from school. "How come you didn't drill with everyone else?"

"I didn't feel like it."

"You can't drill, can you?"

"Yes, I can . . . when I want to."

"Why don't you be our secretary?" Deja says quickly. *And too brightly,* Nikki thinks.

"Why would I want to be secretary?"

"You can take our attendance and stuff," Deja says.

"There's only six of us. Why would we need to have *attendance?*"

"Well, you can also take notes . . . on how everyone is drilling."

"How can I drill and take notes at the same time?"

Deja sighs. "You'll be doing secretary stuff *instead* of drilling."

"Why can't I drill?"

"Because you don't know how," Deja blurts out.

"That's not fair," Nikki says. "I don't want to be secretary." Why is she protesting? She doesn't even like drilling.

Deja lets two whole days pass before she brings up the subject again. After school on Friday, just as they're about to go into their separate houses, she says, "Nikki, you're messing us up 'cause you just can't drill. Why can't you be—"

"I'm not going to be anything!" Nikki says, cutting her off. "And, anyway, I don't want to be in the stupid club anymore!" She hadn't meant to say that. It just came out. And since she can't put the words back into her mouth, she's glad she's in front of her house because then she gets to stomp up her stairs and slam the door behind her.

8

Flea-Market Day

The last Sunday of the month is flea-market day. Auntie Dee always takes Nikki along, which gives Nikki's mom and dad a chance to go out to breakfast, *alone.* Nikki wakes up in a good mood. Now that she's had a day to think about it, she decides she *will* be secretary. She won't have to drill and she'll be able to tell everyone what they're doing wrong. When Deja brings it up, she'll pretend to think about it, then she'll agree.

Nikki looks out the window to see if Deja is coming up the walk yet. There's Bobby, dragging out the lawn mower. He cuts the lawn every Sunday morning.

Finally, Deja appears with Bear and crosses

the small strip of grass between their two houses. Nikki runs out to the porch.

"Look, Nikki," Deja says, showing her the coins in her palm. "Look how much money I have to spend at the flea market." Nikki counts the coins. Fifty-three cents. Deja digs in her pocket. "Plus I have all of this." She pulls out four wrinkled dollar bills. "I've been saving my allowance. How much do you have?"

"Nothing. I didn't save my allowance, and my mother won't give me any more." Nikki sighs. "She said I need to learn the value of a dollar."

"I'll buy you something," Deja says generously. She lifts up Bear. "I'm going to bring Bear with us."

Nikki and Deja follow Auntie Dee to the car. They sit in the car with Bear between them. When they get to the flea market, they each hold Bear by an arm. They decide to go to the knickknack table first. Nikki puts a doily on her head.

"How do I look, Deja?" she asks, happy that their argument is behind them.

"Funny," Deja says.

Deja finds salt and pepper shakers shaped

like pineapples. "I'm going to buy these," she says.

"What are you going to do with them?" Nikki asks. She's glad Deja doesn't seem mad at her for what she said on Friday.

"I'm going to put them on my shelf and look at them. They're for looking at."

"Mmm," Nikki says. She thinks they're meant to hold salt and pepper and be placed on a kitchen table.

Deja holds her shakers in one hand. She holds Bear's arm with the other. They go to a table that has candles that smell like fruit. Nikki and Deja carry Bear around the table. Sometimes they stop to smell the candles. Deja spies a yummy-looking lemon one. "I'm going to buy this," she says.

"What are you going to do with it?" Nikki asks.

"I'm going to put it beside my shakers. It's pretty, and I want to be able to look at it."

Nikki doesn't say anything.

Deja buys the candle, and the candle lady puts it in a bag. Now Deja has the candle in the bag and the salt and pepper shakers.

They see the cotton-candy stand.

"Hold Bear," Deja says, "while I get us some cotton candy."

Nikki takes Bear, but she doesn't really want to. It's different when they're both holding Bear. But now she has Bear on her own. Carrying a stuffed animal by herself might make her look like a baby. And anyway, why hasn't Deja mentioned anything about her being secretary of the Drill Team Club? Maybe Deja's waiting for Nikki to bring it up. Nikki doesn't want to. If Deja doesn't say anything, then she won't, either.

Nikki watches Deja buy one cone of cotton candy and then take a big bite out of it. She skips back to Nikki, her mouth rimmed in sticky pink sugar.

"Where's mine?" Nikki asks.

"The man only had enough syrup to make one. He's waiting for someone to bring him some more." Deja takes another big bite then holds the cotton candy out to Nikki.

Nikki can't help but take a bite. She makes sure it is a small bite, though. She's beginning to feel pouty. Deja has bought things like a grownup, and she hasn't even brought up the club. "Do you want Bear back?" Nikki asks.

"No, you can hold Bear," Deja says, then runs ahead to catch up with Auntie Dee.

Nikki follows with Bear. She really doesn't like carrying Bear alone. Who does Deja think she is, walking ahead, as if Nikki is her maid?

They walk along. Sometimes Auntie Dee stops to look at things she might buy. Sometimes she passes a table without stopping.

Finally, they get to the table with all kinds of strange toys on it. It's Deja's favorite spot. She likes looking at toys you can't find in the toy store. Deja runs around the table, then picks up a robot that can be made into a space ship.

"I wish I had enough money for this. I would buy it."

"But that's a boy toy," Nikki says.

"A girl can play with it, too," Deja replies.

Nikki sees a tiny tea set. She sets Bear on a table nearby and picks up a tiny cup and saucer. She pretends to sip from it.

"Look at this tiny cup and saucer," she says. "I wish I had the money to get it."

Deja looks over at Nikki. "You should have brought money. Everyone knows the flea market is the place to buy."

Nikki wonders if Deja remembers she told

her she would buy her something. Maybe Deja is waiting to see if there's something else she'll want.

They go to the quilt table and then the lamp table. They go to the old-books table, then they go to the plants table. Finally, they start for the car. Deja's arms are full of the odds and ends she's bought. Nikki's remembering Deja's promise to buy her something, a promise Deja didn't keep.

Bear Is Lost

Auntie Dee carries a lamp. When they get to the car, she puts her new lamp between Nikki and Deja.

"Don't let this fall," she says.

Deja looks around for Bear. "Where's Bear?" she asks Nikki.

Nikki looks at Deja. She doesn't know. She left Bear . . . somewhere. But she can't remember where.

"Did you leave Bear?"

"I didn't leave him. I forgot him."

"I think you left him," Deja says. "On purpose."

"I did not."

"You did."

"I said I didn't."

"I think you did it on purpose because you're not in the club anymore," Deja says in a loud voice.

Nikki opens her mouth to speak, but nothing comes out. *Not in the club anymore!* She was supposed to be secretary. What happened to her being secretary? Deja is acting this way on purpose. She knew Nikki was going to tell her she'd decided to be secretary after all. She's just doing these things to be mean.

"We'll go back and get Bear," Auntie Dee says.

Nikki doesn't care if they never find stupid Bear.

Deja starts to cry, as if she believes Nikki would be so mean that she would leave Bear on purpose. Nikki doesn't know why Deja is being such a crybaby. If Deja cared so much, she should have carried Bear herself.

"We'll just go back to all the places we stopped at," Auntie Dee says.

Deja doesn't walk with Nikki. She keeps up with Auntie Dee and leaves Nikki behind.

They go to the indoor-plants stall. "Have you seen a brown bear with shiny brown eyes?" Deja asks the plant lady. She shrugs. They walk around the plants on the table and through all the tall ones. No Bear.

They go to the old-books table. They walk around the table. Nikki walks right behind Deja, but Deja pretends she's not there.

They look under the table. No Bear.

Deja goes to the toy place with all the strange toys. Nikki follows. "Have you seen a brown bear with shiny brown eyes?" Deja asks.

The man doesn't understand. "We don't sell no toy bears."

Deja sighs and walks away slowly, dragging her toes in the dirt. Then she turns to Nikki. "You don't look sorry, Nikki, that you lost my favorite stuffed animal."

Nikki doesn't say anything. She *isn't* sorry. Not even a little bit. She bets Deja isn't all that upset, either. She's just trying to make Nikki feel extra bad. She's probably getting tired of Bear. She's probably feeling too old for Bear. She's probably really glad Bear was lost.

"What's that?" Auntie Dee says, pointing to a fuzzy leg poking out from under a pile of baby quilts on the quilt table.

"You hid Bear," Deja says.

"I didn't hide him, I put him down."

"Why didn't you pick him up?"

"I forgot."

"On purpose."

"Enough," Auntie Dee says. "We have Bear now. So let's be happy."

Back in the car, Auntie Dee places Bear between Nikki and Deja on the back seat along with her lamp.

"Homeward bound," she says.

Nikki and Deja say nothing to each other all the way home. Each looks out her own window instead.

Finally, they reach Fulton Street. Auntie Dee parks the car and reaches into the back seat for her lamp. "Come on," she says. Nikki and Deja climb out of the car. Deja runs up the stairs with all of her bags and Bear. She doesn't look back. Nikki watches her for a few seconds, then climbs the stairs to her own house and goes inside.

Later that night before she drifts off to sleep, after the lights are out, Nikki looks out her window at Deja's bedroom window. She wonders just where in Deja's room she has decided to put her candle and her salt and pepper shakers.

10

Not Speaking

*E*very morning, Deja comes for Nikki, since they walk in that direction to school. On Monday, Nikki waits only a little while for Deja to ring her bell. When the big hand is on the two and the little hand is on the eight, Nikki walks out the front door toward school. She doesn't see Deja until they line up on the yard in their line-up place. For some reason, Mr. Brown is there. He walks them to their classroom. *Where is Ms. Shelby?* everyone wonders.

"Your teacher is out sick today, class, so you'll be having a substitute." Just as Mr. Brown says this, a man who looks too young to be a teacher rushes into the room.

"Sorry I'm late, Mr. Brown. I went to the wrong classroom."

"They're all yours," Mr. Brown says as he leaves.

The substitute puts his bag on Ms. Shelby's desk. He writes his name on the board: *Mr. Rob*. Then he turns around and looks at the class. Everyone looks back. Nikki frowns. Her mother is completely against teachers using their first names. In kindergarten when she had Miss Melissa, her mother insisted that Nikki call her teacher Miss Putter. Most of the time, she didn't.

"You may go to your seats," Mr. Rob says.

"He uses his first name," someone whispers to Nikki. It's Antonia. She's wearing a denim dress and slick black boots. Antonia follows Nikki and settles in the empty desk behind her. It's Richard White's desk. He's absent.

"That's not your seat, Antonia."

"It is today," she says, smiling slyly.

Nikki feels a little thrill shoot through her. That's right—Mr. Rob doesn't know anything. Everybody can sit wherever they want.

Mr. Rob has Deja pass out the morning journals, even though she's not the journal

monitor. Deja looks very pleased. Mr. Rob doesn't notice that she gives everyone their journals before finally giving Nikki hers. But Nikki notices, and she's furious. Mr. Rob has Ralph pass out the pencils. On the board he writes, *Yesterday*.

"Write about yesterday," he says. "Tell me everything."

Nikki opens her journal and puts the date on the top line.

"You and Deja have a drill club, huh?" Antonia whispers.

"I guess so," Nikki says. She doesn't want to tell Antonia about all the complications. She suspects Antonia would like that.

"I want to be in it," she says.

"Deja already has all the girls she wants." Nikki looks down at her paper. Yesterday she went to the flea market and she accidentally misplaced stupid Bear. She doesn't want to write about that. She could write about last night, instead. What happened last night? Oh, yeah, her mother fixed tacos and her father ate four. Then her mother said that was too many for someone who was watching his waistline.

Antonia interrupts Nikki's train of thought with "Ask Deja if I can be in it."

Nikki turns to Antonia and blurts out, "I'm not even in that stupid drill club anymore!" She wishes immediately that she could take it back. Too late.

Antonia's eyes sparkle. "How come?" she asks.

"I hear talking," Mr. Rob says, standing up from Ms. Shelby's chair. "Let's get back to work." He may look young, but he doesn't act young, Nikki decides. She looks over at Deja, who's writing furiously. Deja doesn't even like to write. What could she be writing about?

Maybe she's writing all about how she was

mean to her best friend and blamed her best friend for losing her favorite stuffed animal, even though it wasn't even her best friend's fault.

"Then *we* can have a club," Antonia whispers.

Nikki looks over at Deja again. "What kind of club?" she whispers back to Antonia.

"A club that everyone will want to be in. But we can decide who." She bends her head back over her writing. Mr. Rob is looking right at them.

When the bell rings for recess, Mr. Rob says only those who've written a page can go out. Mr. Rob has them show him their work before dropping it in the basket on Ms. Shelby's desk. Nikki has written only eight lines, so she decides to write big so she can get to the end of the page before missing too much recess.

Deja jumps up out of her seat and holds her full page up for Mr. Rob to see. She holds it in a way so that Nikki can see as well. Before she walks out the door, she looks back at Nikki with a little smile on her face. Nikki can't believe Deja is finished before she is.

She still has five more lines to fill up. She writes big until they're filled, then turns in her journal.

Outside, Nikki takes her time walking over to Antonia. She can't help looking toward the handball court. Deja and Melinda and ChiChi and Keisha and Rosario are in the middle of their drill routine. Nikki can hear their voices. There are some girls from Mr. Beaumont's class and even some from the fourth grade watching. Antonia runs over to Nikki and says, "They're really good."

"Yeah."

"Are you going to be in my club or not?"

Nikki thinks. One club is better than no club. "I guess," she says.

From across the yard, Nikki sees Deja watching this exchange. She watches Deja almost miss a step and mess up the routine.

11

Antonia's Red Sucker Club

The next day Nikki and Deja manage not to walk to school together again. When Nikki hears Deja's front door slam and her footsteps clomping down the porch steps, she counts to fifty. Then she eases out her own front door and starts for school. She can see Deja almost at the end of the block. When she sees Deja look back, Nikki walks extra slowly so she won't catch up with her. Nikki's glad she isn't in the Drill Team Club. *Who needs Deja?* she tells herself as she walks a safe distance behind, all the way to school.

Mr. Rob is back. Nikki wonders how Ms. Shelby got sick. She keeps a plastic bottle of hand sanitizer on her desk, and in the morning, while everyone's writing in their journals, she walks down each row and squirts a little in each person's palm.

"Ms. Shelby must be really sick," Antonia says as she slips in line behind Nikki. That's not her place. It's Rosario's place. But Rosario simply gets in line behind Antonia. If she argues, Mr. Brown might notice talking in their line, and Room Ten's chances of winning the pizza party will be ruined. Suddenly, a pushing match breaks out in Mr. Beaumont's line. The kids in Ms. Shelby's class keep their heads facing straight ahead, but they try to roll their eyes as far to the left and Mr. Beaumont's line as possible.

The sound of an escalating argument between two students in Mr. Beaumont's line is a wonderful thing. Mr. Brown makes a note on his clipboard, and Mr. Beaumont steps in to break it up.

Everyone knows that little spat has put Room Ten in first place. Now, if Antonia can just keep her mouth shut and follow line rules for two more days, Room Ten might win the pizza party.

On the way into the classroom, Antonia slips a sucker into Nikki's hand. It is bright red and cube shaped. Nikki puts it in her pocket.

Later, when they are at their cubbies in the back of the classroom, Nikki asks Antonia, "Why did you give me that sucker?"

"'Cause you're in the Red Sucker Club. I'm president, and you can be vice-president." Antonia puts away her backpack and lunch box. "Each day, at recess, we decide who gets a sucker. We'll choose just four girls out of the whole school. Two for you, and two for me. My grandmother lets me have anything I want— and she bought me a whole bag of red suckers. Next week I'll have her buy me green suckers, then we'll have the Green Sucker Club. And the week after that, the Purple Sucker Club."

Nikki sees Deja look back over her shoulder at the cubbies, then up at the board, where Mr. Rob is writing that day's topic for their journals. In big letters he writes, *What I Like to Do After School.* Nikki goes to her desk and opens her journal.

The Red Sucker Club turns out to be fun. At recess, Nikki walks over to one of the girls from

Mr. Beaumont's class and—as Antonia instructed her—says, "I now admit you into the exclusive Red Sucker Club."

Everyone around them stops playing and watches with their mouths hanging open. Nikki taps the girl on the forehead with the sucker and then holds it out to her. "You are a member for today."

The girl reaches slowly for the sucker and says, "Thanks."

The same thing happens when she interrupts Felicity just as she's getting ready to sock the tetherball. Everyone stops and looks at Nikki—even Deja and her entire drill club. Suddenly, Nikki likes being the one in charge. *It's fun*, she decides.

By lunch recess, the entire third grade is talking about the Red Sucker Club. Everyone is latching on to the mystery of it: the fact that members change every day and no one can know who will be in it. It is completely up to the whims of President Antonia and Vice-President Nikki.

"Your dumb Red Sucker Club is stupid!" Deja yells up at Nikki's window after school.

Nikki looks out. Deja's face is pinched and mean.

"Who thought of it? You or stupid Antonia?"

"You're just mad because you're not in it!" Nikki yells back.

"So? Who wants to be in that club, anyway?"

"Everybody."

"Well, the Drill Team Club—the one you're *not* in—can buy their own suckers!"

"Buy them, then!" Nikki yells, and slams her window shut.

Nikki laughs. Deja is probably in shock. She probably can't believe that Nikki just slammed the window on her—that Nikki cut off the argument just when she was getting started. Nikki imagines Deja stomping into the kitchen to make herself a peanut butter and jelly sandwich. Deja likes to eat when she's mad. She imagines her standing at the sink with steam coming out of her ears. Nikki laughs again.

12

No More Clubs

Ms. Shelby is back! She has a red nose and a cough, but she's there at the line-up place in the morning. So the day is off to a good start. However, in regard to the Red Sucker Club, things don't go the way Antonia predicted. Nikki knows she shouldn't even be surprised. Felicity from Mrs. Miller's class has started her own Purple Sucker Club. She hasn't even bothered with a vice-president, and she's bestowing suckers on too many kids. Nikki, who has two new red suckers to bestow on two lucky members of the day, is not invited to be a member of the Purple Sucker Club. And when she gives one of the two suckers to Taylor from Mr. Beaumont's class, Taylor pulls a purple sucker out of her pocket and says, "Wow, I'm in the Red Sucker Club *and* the Purple Sucker Club!"

Nikki considers snatching her sucker back but then decides to let her keep it. She and Antonia hadn't planned on someone starting their own sucker club and making the Red Sucker Club not even special. Before Nikki bestows her second sucker on Carlos from her own class, she asks him, "Are you in the Purple Sucker Club? You can't have it if you're already in the Purple Sucker Club."

"I'm not," Carlos says. He doesn't wait for the official tap on the forehead. He snatches the sucker out of her hand and runs off.

That afternoon, Mr. Brown puts a halt to everything. His big booming voice comes over the intercom just as Ms. Shelby is writing ten spelling words on the board for the class to use in a story:

"It has come to my attention that someone is bringing candy to school and passing it out on the schoolyard at each recess."

Nikki sees Deja look over at her with eyes widened to big circles. Several of the other students turn to look at Nikki, and then Antonia. Antonia looks cool and calm, Nikki thinks, and

that makes her angry. She's surprised to see the look of concern on Deja's face, since they haven't been best friends for almost three whole days.

"This is going to stop, now. I want no more reports of candy being distributed in the play yard. The rules are: No candy at school!" Then Mr. Brown raises his voice to announce the last part. *"If it's brought to my attention that this behavior continues, the guilty person's class will be disqualified from the pizza party."*

Everyone flinches at this. Several kids turn frowning, accusing faces toward Nikki. A few turn toward Antonia. But it seems that most of the class is looking at Nikki.

Nikki's face feels hot, but Antonia isn't even paying attention. She's busy coloring her nails with green marker.

"Teachers, please be mindful. Let me know as soon as you're aware that this is continuing."

There's a bit of static, then silence. The class has never been more quiet. Everyone waits for Ms. Shelby to fuss at them. Then Ralph pipes up with, "You're going to get us in trouble, Nikki!"

Suddenly, Nikki hears Deja say, "What's your problem, Ralph? Why are you picking on just Nikki?"

Nikki has been biting her tongue to keep from crying, she's so embarrassed. She looks at Deja with surprise. She can't believe Deja is taking up for her.

Ralph opens his mouth to speak, but Ms. Shelby steps in. "That's quite enough. We're going to forget about this. But if I hear any more reports of candy at school"—she calmly walks over to Antonia's desk and holds out her hand for the green marker—"phone calls will be made to parents."

Antonia caps the marker and puts it in Ms. Shelby's hand. She rolls her eyes and sticks out her lower lip.

Then Ms. Shelby adds, "Oh, and Antonia, you need to stay after school so we can discuss disrespectful behavior."

Antonia sighs as loud as she can. Everyone is stunned that Antonia would *dare* roll her eyes at Ms. Shelby. Nikki wonders how she could have let Antonia lead her into breaking a school rule in the first place. She looks over at Deja, who looks at Nikki at the same time. Deja smiles a very tiny smile. Nikki smiles back. Deja took up for her.

13

Friends Again

After school, Nikki sees Deja walking slowly. But this time she thinks it's not to keep from catching up to Nikki, it's so Nikki can catch up with her. Finally, Nikki comes up right behind Deja. Then she's alongside her.

"Hi, Nikki," she says.

"Hi, Deja." Nikki looks straight ahead. They walk in silence for a while.

"Auntie Dee is letting me make chocolate chip cookies after I do my homework. You want to help?" she asks quickly.

"Okay," Nikki says. After a moment, she adds, "And thanks for taking up for me, Deja."

"You're welcome. Wanna do homework together?" Deja asks.

* 71 *

"Okay." Nikki's relieved that Deja isn't saying anything about the silly Red Sucker Club.

"Come over in fifteen minutes," Deja says.

When Nikki gets there, Deja has the squeeze tube of refrigerator cookie dough on the table and a greased cookie sheet. Auntie Dee has already turned on the oven. As soon as they finish their homework, they can get started.

"One page of subtraction and one page of multiplication. Ugh," Deja says. They settle at the kitchen table and pull their homework out of their book bags. "What's seven times nine?"

"Sixty-three," Nikki says. "You have to learn your facts, Deja."

"Okay. What's six times seven?"

"Forty-two." Nikki is silent for a while and then says, "Deja? I'll be secretary if you still want me to be."

"Secretary of what?"

"Of the Drill Team Club," Nikki says.

"Oh—we broke that up."

Surprised, Nikki asks, "You broke it up? Why?"

Deja is busy counting on her fingers. She writes down an answer and says, "Nobody was getting along. Rosario is bossy. Melinda thinks she can make up routines when she can't. . . ." Deja pauses to erase her answer and write something else. "It's too much trouble."

Nikki thinks about this. "So what kind of club do you want to have?"

"No club. Why do we have to have a club? We can have fun without a club."

"Yeah," Nikki agrees. "And having a club just to keep people out is kind of mean." She waits for Deja's agreement, but Deja keeps doing her homework.

After a while, Deja says, "Nikki, you think we'll win the pizza party?"

"I think we will. Mr. Beaumont's class just got that really bad boy from another school, and he has a hard time following rules."

"What kind of pizza should we ask for?" Deja says.

They both think for a moment, then say at the same time: "Barbequed chicken with mushrooms and olives and three cheeses!" They slap palms and laugh and laugh, for no other reason than that it's so much fun to laugh.

Later, after they've made the cookies, they go out to the porch with two cookies each, to watch Fulton Street before the sun goes down. Deja sits on the top step, and Nikki sits on the bottom step. Nikki takes a big bite of warm cookie. Deja will probably nibble on hers, Nikki thinks. She likes to be the last one to have something yummy to eat.

It feels good to be sitting on the steps together. A screen door slams. Vianda walks out, cradling her cat, Bianca. She waves at Nikki and Deja, then sits down on her own steps, just to pet her cat and enjoy the evening, it seems.

"Bianca is Bear's best friend," Deja says.

Nikki looks at Deja. She's serious.

"Deja, a cat can't be a stuffed bear's best friend."

"Yes, it can, and Bianca is Bear's."

Nikki laughs. This is why she likes Deja so much. Deja is . . . different.

Mr. Robinson is watering his front lawn, but all's quiet at Bobby's. His car is not in his driveway.

"I like our street, don't you, Nikki?" Deja says.

"Yeah, it's the best street in the world," Nikki agrees.

And the best thing about Fulton Street, Nikki thinks—and hopes that Deja is thinking, too—is that they each live next door to their very best friend.